TAD LINCOLN AND THE GREEN UMBRELLA

TAD LINCOLN
And
the Green Umbrella

By Margaret Friskey

Illustrations by Darrell Wiskur

CHILDRENS PRESS, CHICAGO

CONTENTS

THIS UMBRELLA BELONGS TO ABRAHAM LINCOLN

1 TAD'S SECRET

It was somewhat oversize, the big, green, cotton umbrella. It stood inside the door of the frame house on Eighth Street. There was nothing to distinguish it from the other umbrellas that bloomed over the wooden sidewalks of Springfield, Illinois, on a rainy day, nothing at all, except the large name tag that was sewed securely to the inside. It said in bold, black ink: THIS UMBRELLA BELONGS TO ABRAHAM LINCOLN.

It stood there now, with its long neck crooked as though trying to overhear the conversation in the Lincoln dining room. There was a lull that comes before the storm breaks.

Robert Lincoln in his best clothes was eating in haste, because he was going to a ball at the home of Ninian Edwards. Robert was already assuming some of the manners of a Harvard man. Willie, with his legs wrapped around the legs of his chair, ate his venison steak and hominy with the enthusiastic appetite of a ten-year-old. Mr. and Mrs. Lincoln faced each other across the kerosene lamp that lighted their supper table. Both of them were silently aware of the light flickering on eight-year-old Tad's vacant chair.

"He has absolutely no sense of time," said Mrs. Lincoln. "He knows we have supper at six o'clock."

"Boys his age have no more sense of time than a pig has feathers."

"You are too easy on him, Mr. Lincoln, that's the trouble. Boys have to be taught to mind. You have always let the boys run wild all over the surrounding country like Indians."

"Boys need freedom to grow."

"Yes, that's what you always say; but Willie and Robert have sense enough to come home for their meals."

"They probably take after their mother's side of the family."

A sudden gust of wind whipped aside the lace curtains at the window. The lamp flickered, smudging the side of the chimney with soot.

"It's going to storm," said Mrs. Lincoln in alarm. She had always been afraid of storms.

"I believe you're right, Mother," said Mr. Lincoln, pushing back his chair. "I must go out and milk Blackie."

"But Tad?"

"I'll find Tad. Don't worry."

"Take your umbrella. It may rain before you get back. And, Mr. Lincoln, please hurry. I don't like to be alone in a storm, you know." She always called her husband Mr. Lincoln, not because he was President-elect of the United States, but because it was a habit with her.

Mr. Lincoln unwound his long legs and stood up. "Willie," he said, "where do you think Tad is?"

"He's probably running for home like a jackrabbit," said Robert, "now that it's blowing up a storm."

"I bet he went over to see Miss Sophia's goat," said Willie. "He goes to see that old goat every day."

"Um." Mr. Lincoln stood with his big hands gripping the back of his chair. "Never saw a boy want anything like Tad wants a goat. Mother, would you have any objections to—"

"Objections! Mr. Lincoln, I'll have no goat around this place. Goats, umph! Horrid creatures! They smell, and they have dreadful dispositions."

"Tad has even been taking the matter up with the Lord from time to time. But if you say no goat, I guess the Lord can't possibly do anything about it."

Mr. Lincoln turned from the table. He stopped to pick up his umbrella and a lantern. Then he made his way to the barn.

Inside the barn the lantern didn't give much light, but it was enough to show that Blackie was restless in her stall. It also revealed young Tad Lincoln sitting on the partition of the stall. He had torn his black stockings and was generally disheveled.

Mr. Lincoln picked up the three-legged stool. He carried it around to Blackie's right side and sat down. For a while there was the quiet rhythm of milk hitting the pail.

"Whoa, Blackie," said Mr. Lincoln. "Whoa! Quiet there. Seems sometimes that Blackie can't rest until she plants one of her hind feet in my pants pocket."

He talked without looking up. It was as though the

barn was the most natural place in the world for Tad to spend his supper hour.

Tad laughed. His troubles all faded in the warm glow of his father's good nature. He held out a handful of corn to Jasper, his pet crow. Jasper ate what was offered and searched Tad's pockets for more.

For some time there was no sound in the barn except Blackie's restless stomping and the sound of the milk hitting the side of the pail.

Finally Tad spoke. "You don't like fights, do you, Papa?"

"I loath fights." Mr. Lincoln continued milking. The pail was almost full. Then he added, "But sometimes, Tad, you run up against something, and you have to fight. Why, when I was a little fellow going to school in Indiana, I met a boy—he was bigger than I was—and he was putting red hot coals on the back of a turtle. That helpless turtle was suffering. I asked the boy to stop, but he wouldn't, so I hit him."

"You did? Did he hit you back?"

"Um. He did, indeed. That black eye he gave me is one that I will long remember. However, the turtle got away."

"I had to have a fight, too."

"You did? I thought perhaps you had had a slight run-in with a gooseberry bush," said Mr. Lincoln. "Would you like to tell me about it?"

"Well." Tad sat kicking his button shoes against the side of the stall as he reflected. "You know Miss Sophia's chestnut horse?"

"Yes. About as thin as the shadow of a pigeon that had starved to death."

"He's a good horse! And Miss Sophia was brushing him and washing his white feet—he has four you know. She was getting him all cleaned up, 'cause she wanted to take him to the sale tomorrow and sell him for a good price. And Caleb Norton was standing there."

"He's a sight bigger than you are."

"That was the trouble. He was standin' there, making fun of that good horse. Then when she had him all ready for the sale, Caleb shot him with a slingshot, and he ran away. So I hit Caleb, and—and he hit me back." Tad's lower lip quivered slightly. He blinked a couple of times and stopping talking.

"That isn't too serious. That horse will come back to the barn."

"Sure, but shucks, it's rainin' and he'll be covered all over with mud. Miss Sophia can't ever get him ready for the sale in time"—Tad hesitated—"by herself."

"Oh, so you're going to help her?"

"That's right."

"Well, I can't see anything wrong with that."

Tad rubbed his leg for a minute as he thought about the injustice that can be done by one boy who has the inclinations of a bully.

"And there's one more thing about this Caleb Norton," Tad said.

"What's that?"

"He called me a sissy for helping Miss Sophia." Tad's voice rose.

"He did?"

"Yes. But I like Miss Sophia. She's my friend."

"I know. Tell me this, son. If I call Blackie's tail a leg, how many legs will Blackie have?"

"Why, five, of course."

"Wrong. You can't make a tail a leg by calling it one."

"Then I'm not a sissy?"

"Certainly not. You go on being what you want to be and you will accomplish what you set out to do. Nobody can stop you."

Mr. Lincoln straightened up on the stool and stretched his long arms to get the kinks out of the muscles. Blackie took this opportunity to kick. The pail somersaulted through the air and delivered four quarts of milk right in the middle of Mr. Lincoln's shirt front. It splashed over his coat sleeves and ran down his pant legs into his slippers. Mr. Lincoln jumped up off the stool. He brushed himself off as best he could, muttering to himself. There was certainly something tenacious about four quarts of milk, once it settled on you.

"You should let me milk Blackie," cried Tad, jumping off his perch and picking up the empty pail. "Jimminy, all I get to do around here is take out the garbage and beat the rugs."

Mr. Lincoln took off his slippers and dumped the milk out of them and handed them to Tad.

"Come on, son," he said, "we'd better be getting back to the house."

He opened the barn door. A November drizzle had set in, and the wind was piercing cold.

Mr. Lincoln stooped to roll up his pant legs a couple of turns. He held the green umbrella out the

door and opened it. Then he hoisted Tad to his
shoulder and started for the house, barefooted.

The kitchen door flew open, and Tad and his father
were caught in the pool of light that flooded out of
the doorway. Mrs. Lincoln's shrill voice cut across the
backyard of the frame house on Eighth Street,
sharper than the razor-edge of the November wind.

"Mr. Lincoln!" she shrieked. "Look at you, and you
the most important man in all this country! Barefooted, as I live. What if some of the respectable citi-
zens of Springfield should see you now? Whatever
would they think? You—going to Washington in a
few months to be the President of these United States
—standing there with mud between your toes, and

milk all over you from head to foot, as though you didn't have sense enough to get along with a cow. And Tad! Merciful heavens, what am I ever going to do with you two?"

Mr. Lincoln stood still in his tracks, mustering as much dignity as he could under the circumstances. He looked sadly down the long, spattered expanse of his legs to his bare feet, and to the cold mud that oozed up between his toes. "A touch of nature makes the whole world kin," he quoted. "I have always held that even great men should keep the common touch. And come to think of it, Mother, I do not believe my election was ever announced to Blackie. I am sure the nominating committee forgot her. Don't blame the poor cow for being uninformed."

"Oh, Mr. Lincoln," said Mrs. Lincoln laughing, "you are the most delightful man I ever knew, and the worst one to manage. Come in here, both of you, and get cleaned up before I lose my temper."

She left the doorway and went to put a kettle of water on the stove. Two kettles.

Tad leaned over until his face was close to his father's ear. "I forgot to tell you something special," he said.

"What's that, my young man?"

"Miss Sophia said if I help her with her horse, Jeff, and ride him to the sale for her and get a good price— do you know what?"

"I don't know what," said Mr. Lincoln. His imagination had few limitations, but he was afraid to hazard a guess.

"She's going to give me her goat!"

2 A HORSE OF ANOTHER COLOR

The November sun slanted through the windows of the schoolroom. It fell like a spotlight on the fat, little stove with its short, bowed legs.

It was warm and stuffy in the small room. There was the drone of voices as the pupils of the third grade took turns reading aloud to the rest of the class. They were an average class of boys and girls from the new American Middle West. Although most of their reading lessons, both in prose and poetry, admonished them to behave nicely, as a group, they were not unduly affected by it.

Daisy Diller's small voice piped up and down as she read the day's reading lesson from Watt's verses, *Against Quarrelling and Fighting*.

> Let dogs delight to bark and bite,
>   For God has made them so;
> Let bears and lions roar and fight
>   For 'tis their nature too.
> But, children, you should never let
>   Your angry passions rise;
> Your little hands were never made to
>   Tear each other's eyes.

Tad idly felt the tender spot around his right eye. It had been slightly discolored by Caleb Norton's powerful jab, but so far no one had noticed it.

The droning voice continued, and Tad's mind wandered. He slumped deeper and deeper in his seat. Finally his eyes were on a level with the border at the top of the page. He looked at the stove with drowsy, half-closed eyes. It seemed almost alive. A thought flashed through his mind. It would be pretty funny if the little stove should start to dance; to twirl and bow, and spin around quickly and kick the teacher in the shin with one of its little iron legs. He looked at the stiff folds of the teacher's alpaca skirt that was backed up by a battery of petticoats. She was pretty well protected, but even so—

Tad smiled to himself and ducked his head behind his reader.

"Thomas Lincoln!" snapped the teacher, rapping sharply on the desk with her long ruler. "Do you see anything funny in Mr. Watt's verse against quarreling and fighting?"

"No, ma'am," said Tad.

"What, then, are you laughing at?"

"Why—er—" Tad was as sober as a cornered possum.

"Stand, please," ordered the teacher, "and come to the front of the room."

Tad hunched himself up in his seat and slid out. He walked toward the front of the room without enthusiasm.

"Now," said the teacher, "you may share your funny secret with all of us."

She quietly folded her hands over her stomach and waited. Her lips smiled, but her piercing eyes seemed to run him through and pin him to the wall.

A thousand things flashed through Tad's mind as he stood there before the class. It was almost four o'clock. School would be out soon. He could run to Miss Sophia's to help her clean up Jeff and still have time to get him to the sale. He could even get home for supper at six o'clock as his mother had strongly suggested. But if he made the teacher mad, he would surely have to stay after school and write the reading lesson on his slate twenty times. Then Miss Sophia wouldn't sell her horse, and he would not get the goat. All in all, he would have a very bad time of it.

The eyes of the room were on him. These third graders regarded Tad with new respect since his father had been elected President. They knew that soon he would be leaving Springfield to ride to Washington on a "sleeper train."

His father, that was it, thought Tad. His father would never get backed into a tight place without having something to say.

Tad shifted his weight from one foot to another. He fumbled with the odds and ends in his pants pockets. Then suddenly, he looked up and grinned.

"I was just thinking about something funny that happened when Papa was learning to read in a little log schoolhouse in Indiana."

"You were? Well"—the teacher relaxed—"it is always interesting to hear stories about your father. Close your books, children. Thomas has a story to tell us before we are dismissed."

"When Papa went to a field school in Indiana," began Tad, "they didn't have any good teachers, like we have." He looked slyly at the teacher. She began to mellow. "They didn't have any books either. Not one single reader book in the whole school. Papa had a Bible at home so he brought that to school and the little boys and girls had to learn to read from that. Oh, the Bible is all right, but as Papa said, the words were awful big for children who were just learning to read."

"Well, yes," said the teacher, "those words would be very difficult."

"One day," continued Tad, "they were standing up reading a story about the three Hebrew children in the fiery furnace. The little fellow that stood next to Papa had yellow hair that stood straight up—he had the verse with the names. He got all mixed up trying to say, ah—to say—"

"Shadrach, Meshach, and Abednego?"

"That's right. He got all mixed up trying to say Shadrach, Meshach, and Abednego. The teacher walloped him with a hickory stick. It smarted so that the little boy sobbed out loud. But the reading lesson went right on. Everybody read a verse and pretty soon it was the little fellow's turn again. He stopped crying and looked at the page through his tears, and then suddenly he screamed.

"'What's the matter with you now?'" asked the teacher.

"'Look there,' cried the boy, pointing to the page, 'there come them same three fellers again!'"

The teacher and the children all laughed at Tad's

story, and with a sense of relief he could see that the rest of the day would be his. He went back to his seat with wings on his feet.

"For tomorrow," said the teacher, "you may do the first ten problems on page fifteen in your arithmetics, and study the next verse about quarrelling and fighting in the Watt's Reader. Class dismissed."

Tad jammed his arms into the sleeves of his wool coat, clapped his cap on his head, tossed the long plaid muffler around his neck a couple of times, and flew out the door.

The fourth graders were already swarming into the yard. Tad caught a glimpse of Caleb Norton. He was surrounded by an interested group of boys and girls. They seemed to be hanging on his every word. Tad frowned slightly. Caleb was not liked much by the other children in his grade, and he usually left school alone with his books slung over his shoulder.

Tad stopped in his tracks to see what was the cause of Caleb's sudden popularity. His eyes opened wide with astonishment as he saw Caleb's right eye. It was almost swollen shut, and the whole side of his face was black-and-blue. Tad took a deep breath that almost popped the buttons off his shirt. Well! Maybe he didn't get the worst of his fight with Caleb, after all. Sissies didn't leave marks like that on the other fellow.

Tad sauntered over to the edge of the interested group. They would sure be glad to hear somebody— even a third grader—had nerve enough to take a poke at a big bully like Caleb.

"Where'd ya get the black eye? Who punched ya? Law, what a wallop!" The voices of the fourth graders

rose around Tad. Pride swelled within him. He felt strong enough at that moment to pick up the world and use it like a marble in a game of chasies.

"Ah, that's nothin'," said Caleb. "That's nothin'. A horse kicked me."

"It did?"

"Sure. Knocked a couple of my teeth loose, too. It was that black mare of Pa's. I was grooming her to take her to the sale this afternoon."

"Nobody gonna want to buy a horse that kicks your teeth out," suggested one little boy in a red woolly coat.

"She's a good horse," declared Caleb. "Lot of spirit. That's all. She'll make all the other horses at the sale look like they was made of wood. Well, I gotta be goin'. Got to go to the sale, you know."

Tad turned and ran out of the school yard. So that was it. So that was why Caleb made Miss Sophia's horse run away and get all muddy and tired out. Well, he'd fix Jeff up so he looked as good as any old black mare that kicked people. He'd . . .

Tad ran around the corner of Diller's Drugstore as fast as he could go. His muffler trailed out behind him like the tail of a kite. His feet beat a tattoo on the boards of the wooden sidewalk. On around Capitol Square he went, and past the big, impressive brick house of his Uncle Ninian. He ran to the edge of town where Miss Sophia lived in a little white cottage with a picket fence around it.

Jasper swooped down and sat on the fence as Tad entered the gate. Tad stopped and held out his hand, and Jasper jumped onto his wrist.

"Say," said Tad, "I forgot to look for you, I had so many things on my mind. Have you been following me all the way from school?"

Jasper ruffled his glossy neck feathers in indignation, and wiped his bill on Tad's sleeve. "Well, come on," said Tad. "We'll go round to Miss Sophia's barn, and you can have some corn. I guess she can spare you a little since she's gonna sell her horse."

They found Miss Sophia in the barn working on Jeff. Jeff was a mess. He was caked with mud. His mane and tail were in a tangle. His white feet were yellow with clay. His beautiful chestnut coat might have been any color.

"He came back last night," said Miss Sophia briefly, as she worked with a brush, "but I couldn't get out here to clean him up 'til just now. I'm glad you've come, Tad."

"I said I would."

"I know. But your family is busy these days. I couldn't expect you to be thinking of me."

Tad pulled up an old chair without a back and stood on it so that he could reach the top of Jeff's neck. He took the brush from Miss Sophia and worked with vigor. Jasper set about looking for grain, with great success. The tangled mane was not improved much by the brush.

Tad jumped down and pumped a pail of water. Water and the brush together did the work. Soon Jeff began to shine. Tad got clean water and scrubbed the horse's four white feet. Miss Sophia pulled the broken chair back out of range of Jeff's restless hooves and sat down with a sigh.

She and Tad talked very little. Their friendship was a solid one, built on a firm foundation of understanding and molasses cookies. There was no time for talk. The sale was at five o'clock.

Finally Tad was ready to go. He lifted the saddle off the nail on the wall, dusted it, and put in on Jeff.

"Want me to sell the saddle with the horse?" asked Tad.

"Saddle won't be worth much without a horse to put it on."

"That's right." Tad shortened the stirrups and picked up the reins in his left hand. He put his left foot in the left stirrup, which was about even with his chin, and pulled himself up. He swung his right leg over the back of the horse and settled in the saddle.

"You're pretty little to go to a sale," said Miss Sophia.

"I'll bring you an offer of fifty dollars for Jeff, or— or I'll never eat another molasses cookie as long as I live. You wait and see."

Jeff walked out of the barn. Tad turned to wave to Miss Sophia standing in the doorway.

"Take good care of the goat for me," he shouted over his shoulder as he and Jeff went through the gate and headed for the market. Jasper flew along from tree to tree with a lot of noise and fuss.

"Go on," said Tad to the crow. "Go on, and catch yourself a few beetles. I've got work to do."

3 JASPER TAKES A RIDE

The market square was humming with activity. There were horses and carts and covered wagons. Buyers were looking over the animals with practiced eyes, studying their conformation, looking at their teeth, feeling the muscles in their legs.

Tad saw Caleb dash into the square on the black mare. Everybody saw him. The mare picked up her feet daintily and tossed her mane. She showed such spirit that Caleb had all he could do to handle her. Caleb's father was there, looking very pleased at the horse's performance.

"Here's a horse that's worth your money," shouted Mr. Norton. The buyers stopped everything to watch Caleb and the horse with admiration.

"Give her a turn around the square," Caleb's father shouted.

The horse reared on her hind legs, spun around a couple of times, and galloped around the square.

"Showing off like a peacock," thought Tad as he came plodding up unnoticed. Poor Jeff was too tired

to show much enthusiasm for the business at hand. His tail drooped, his head sagged down on his neck, and he stumbled along into the middle of the square.

"Hey," said Tad earnestly as he gave a tug at the reins and leaned forward toward the horse's ear. "Step along. They'll think you are nothing but an old bag of bones. Come on, now, toss your head, show a little spirit, and for heaven's sake, pick up your feet!"

Mr. Norton's booming voice rang out across the square again. "If you don't think you're getting a bargain in that little black mare, just take a look at that poor, old chestnut nag over there." He laughed heartily and pointed Jeff out to a prospective buyer.

"Caw! Caw!" cried Jasper from a treetop, where he could keep an eye on the proceedings.

Jeff tossed his head in answer to Jasper.

"That's better," said Tad. "That's being a little

more like yourself. They can't make you an old nag just by calling you one."

The sale went on and on, and the crowd thinned out. Men who had bought new horses led them away or rode off on them. No one had looked twice at Jeff. Tad sat in the saddle wrapped in gloom.

There were still a few people standing around the square. But the only man interested in buying a horse was the one Mr. Norton had cornered. Caleb rode up on the black mare and reined her to a stop before both men.

"Get on," suggested Mr. Norton to the man who was the last customer in sight. "Try her yourself. Spirited, but gentle. Just what a horse should be."

Tad watched the man ride off. He swallowed over a lump in his throat as big as a pumpkin. "Sure," he said to himself, "so gentle he'll probably kick your teeth out at the first chance."

The mare was spinning in circles. Then she reared on her hind legs, almost dumping the rider off in the mud, but he hung on and off they went around the square.

Just then Mr. Lincoln came along with that long stride of his and stopped to watch the show. He wore his high hat which made him seem even taller than six feet four. He held a plaid shawl around his shoulders against the chill of the November day. The horse and rider who had managed to stay together for a wild turn around the square slowed down in front of him.

"Hello, Abe," shouted the fellow from his insecure perch atop the restless horse. "What do you think of this mare as a buy?"

The mare began to dance around like somebody walking barefooted into a bunch of tacks.

"You make me think of an Irishman I saw trying a horse, once," said Abe.

"How's that?"

"Well, that Irishman stayed on until the horse jumped around so that he almost got his hind foot in the stirrup. The Irishman looked around and addressed the rear end of the horse, saying, 'By gorra, if you're gonna git on, I'm gonna git off.' And he did."

The man on the black mare laughed, and so did everybody present, except the Nortons. The rider got off the horse, and handed the reins to Caleb. He forgot about horse buying and made the most of this rare opportunity to talk to his old friend, Abe.

Tad came up on Jeff. "Oh, Papa," he cried, "did you come to help me sell Jeff for Miss Sophia?"

"Well," said Mr. Lincoln, "that isn't what I had in mind. I was sent here by your mother to see that you come home in time for supper."

"This is Tad, my youngest."

"Well, now, I didn't recognize that little fellow. Looks like his pa, too."

"Would you like to try Jeff?" asked Tad brightly. He slipped from the saddle and gave the reins to his father's friend. "Jeff is really a good horse. Quiet and steady, and he doesn't eat too much."

"I'm afraid he's a little too quiet for me. When I want to get someplace I set out for, I want to get there."

"Just try him a minute. He has an easy gait."

"Well," said the man taking the reins and mounting

Jeff. "To please the youngest son of a good story teller, I will ride this lightning bolt around the square." He smiled indulgently to Tad who stood by his father's side, and Jeff began to move.

"If I've grown a beard by the time you get back," said Abe, "it's because I just got a letter from a little girl suggesting that I would have more dignity as President if I had one."

Jeff set out with the slow, mechanical pace of a sleepwalker. They reached the far side of the square and turned to return. Jasper, as though he were getting pretty tired of all the delay, flew down and lit quietly on the horse's back just behind the unsuspecting rider. Jasper often rode this way with Tad. Jeff moved too slowly to suit Jasper so he pecked him sharply. Jasper's tough, old beak dug into Jeff like the business end of a steel drill.

Jeff shot forward like the ball of lead from a Brown Bess musket. He forgot he was tired. He tossed his head. He picked up his feet. He galloped. And with the speed of a highbred racehorse, he headed for Miss Sophia's barn.

Tad left his father and ran after Jeff as fast as he could go. With the sudden departure of their prospective buyer, there was nothing for Caleb Norton and his father to do but go home with their black mare.

Mr. Lincoln chuckled to himself as he went home to supper without Tad. "That old crow!" he said to himself. "I never suspected him of being much account in a business way, but that's one time Jasper did contribute something to the end in view."

4 THE UNWELCOME GOAT

There were important guests at the frame house on Eighth Street. The small parlor swarmed with them. Mr. John Hay and Mr. John Nicolay were there. They were going to Washington as secretaries to Mr. Lincoln. The governor of Indiana was there and the governor of Massachusetts, and many others who had come a long way to talk to the man who would be inaugurated as President in March.

The supper dishes had been cleared away and the round dining-room table was covered with a dark cloth that hung almost to the floor.

Mrs. Lincoln, with the gracious manner of a southern hostess, stood in the hall to greet the important callers as they arrived and make them welcome. She wore her new black silk dress with the billowing skirt that rustled when she moved. Her round face with its clear skin was framed by her straight black hair which was parted in the middle and combed down across her ears and into a neat roll at the back of her neck. She wore no jewelry because she had none. She was a plump person with the sleek well-groomed look of a polished apple. She held her head high and moved with the air of a great lady.

Mrs. Lincoln looked around her simple home with an appraising eye. She wished she had a house that was as impressive as her sister's, Mrs. Ninian Edwards. A big brick place with long windows and a cupola. This small house was not grand enough for the President-elect. What must these big men in the country think? Mr. Lincoln didn't seem to mind. He had come in late for supper and had not even changed into his best suit. His rumpled pants looked as though he had slept in them for a week. His collar, which was always too big for him, was anchored to his stiff, white shirt with a large bow tie, slightly crooked. His shoes were the heavy, serviceable, plain-toed ones he wore every day. The heels were caked with mud from his hasty trip across the Springfield streets to get home in time for supper.

He had tossed his stovepipe hat wrong side up in the little rocker, where he could easily reach the important papers that he always carried in the top of it. His worn and ridiculous hat was one of his favorite garments.

And the bookcase in the parlor! Mrs. Lincoln shuddered and turned away. It seemed to bristle like a porcupine with Mr. Lincoln's papers. They poked out of the cubbyholes. Those that he wished to give first attention were tucked helter-skelter behind the glass doors that sheltered the books. Mrs. Lincoln sighed with resignation. She couldn't do any more than she had done.

She glanced with a certain amount of distaste at the sideboard in the corner of the dining room. A large mirror hung over it with fruit pictures on either side. There was that little walnut bracket by the door that held certain breakable bric-a-brac high out of the reach of little hands. What would Washington people think of such a simple room?

The parlor wasn't much better. She had once thought the little twisted-leg table with its embroidered wool cover that stood by the armchair was rather nice. But how small-town it looked now with the governor of Massachusetts drumming his fingers on it! The figured carpet was almost threadbare in the middle of the room where Mr. Lincoln had played horse with the boys for so many hours. How could a woman ever keep a house nice with such a family? The small parlor was blue with cigar smoke, and Mrs. Lincoln sighed as she noticed the gray tendrils curling up and settling in her clean lace curtains.

She sighed again and smiled to herself. It would all be different when they got to Washington. There would be broad staircases and crystal chandeliers, and heavy brocaded curtains that hung from ceiling to floor. She squared her shoulders with determination. She would see to it that her family behaved in keeping with their fine new home, once they go there. Robert and Willie, who had come in and gone quietly to their rooms, would know instinctively what it meant to be the President's children. But Tad . . . well, she would manage Tad, somehow.

She shut her eyes and tried not to listen. Mr. Lincoln was telling these men how he had split fifteen hundred rails for the Widow Miller, to earn his first suit of blue jeans. The jeans were so tight at the bottom and so short that they cut a blue ring in each leg that you could see today. What must these people think of his simple past?

"There is a lot of trouble brewing, Mr. Lincoln," said Mr. Hay. "You may even find you have a war on your hands when you get to Washington."

"I sincerely hope not," replied Mr. Lincoln. The lines deepened in his gaunt face. "I sincerely hope not. Nothing was ever really gained by appealing anything from the ballot to the bullet."

"How do you feel about being President, anyway?" put in Mr. Nicolay. "Sometimes I have a feeling you would rather stay on right here and be a country lawyer."

"How do I feel about being President? I'll tell you. Once there was a fellow here who was being ridden out of town on a rail by the angry citizenry. Some-

body in the crowd yelled at him and said, 'Hey, how do you like the ride?' The fellow on the rail replied with what dignity he could muster under the circumstances, 'Well, sir, if it weren't for the honor of the thing, I'd just as soon walk!'"

The men in the smoke-filled room laughed heartily. This fellow Abe certainly could say a lot in one simple story that was right to the point.

Suddenly, above the talk and laughter in the parlor, there arose a terrific noise in the front hall.

The front door flew open. Tad appeared triumphantly in the front hall with his goat by the collar. The goat pranced about, upsetting the green umbrella and kicking over the hatrack. The high hat of the governor of Massachusetts went rolling across the floor. The small hall was filled with a smell that was undeniably goat. When Mrs. Lincoln overcame her shock enough to catch her breath, she shrieked.

"Tad Lincoln!" she screamed so that they could hear her down at Diller's Drugstore. "Tad Lincoln! What are you doing with that horrible creature?"

"Just bringin' him home," said Tad, simply.

"Well, get him out of here. Get him out, this instant!"

"He's mine," said Tad, defiantly.

"You can't bring a goat in here."

"I'll take him to the barn."

"I won't have a goat in the barn, either. Goats! Horrors! He'd be eating the clothes off the line and digging up the garden and smelling up the place for miles around. Get him out of here, do you understand? Get him out! Take him back where he came from. I'll have no—"

Mr. Lincoln could see that Mrs. Lincoln was close to tears. It had been a busy day for her. This goat in the hall was just one thing too many. Silence had fallen in the crowded parlor. Mr. Lincoln walked quietly into the hall. He opened the front door and led Tad and his goat outside.

"I should have told you that Mother wouldn't let you keep a goat here. I guess I never thought you would really sell that horse for Miss Sophia and get him."

Mr. Lincoln stooped and put his arm around the boy. "Looks like a pretty good goat, too."

"He's a wonderful goat," said Tad. "With whiskers."

The Unwelcome Goat

The man and the boy and the goat went down the walk to the little iron gate in the front fence.

"Tad, my son," said Mr. Lincoln, "I think you'd better take this goat back to Miss Sophia. She'll be pretty lonesome, you know, with Jeff gone, too."

"That's right. I never thought of that."

"He can be yours, but let her keep him for you. He'll be your responsibility, of course. So perhaps we could let her have Blackie, too, when we go away. That would sort of pay her for the trouble."

Tad took a firm grip on the goat's collar again. The two of them went sadly down the street. Mr. Lincoln could tell by the way Tad ducked his head and stumbled along that he was blinded by tears. Turning slowly, Mr. Lincoln walked back into the house to finish up the less important business of the day. His guests had gathered up their scattered hats and were saying farewell to Mrs. Lincoln. One by one they left.

Mr. Lincoln went to his desk. He began to work on some of the papers that cluttered the glass doors of the bookcase. Mrs. Lincoln came into the parlor and with a sigh of exhaustion dropped heavily into the small rocker. There was the distressing crunch of a flattened hat. She jumped to her feet, ready to burst into tears.

Mr. Lincoln stood up, patted her on the shoulder affectionately. Then he picked up his smashed headpiece and remarked, "Madam, I might have told you it wouldn't fit before you tried it on."

"Oh, Mr. Lincoln!" she said, not knowing whether to laugh with him, or to cry. She picked up her rustling skirts with a flourish and swept up the narrow stairs with all the dignity of a President's wife.

5 A HOUSE DIVIDED

Mr. Lincoln worked for some time, but his mind was not wholly on his work. He was unconsciously listening for Tad's return.

At last he heard Tad come in the back door and climb the stairs. Then there were footsteps overhead as Tad moved around his room.

Mr. Lincoln sorted out the papers on his desk. He tucked a few carelessly behind the glass doors of the bookcase and jammed the rest of them into cubbyholes. He picked up his hat and removed the papers in the top of it with some difficulty. He turned the poor broken thing over in his hands a few times, regarding it with affection, and dropped it into the wastebasket. He could still hear Tad's footsteps overhead. Tad was a long time getting into bed.

Mr. Lincoln turned out the lamp and went upstairs. He opened Tad's door a crack and peeked in. The room was in a turmoil. The drawers of the little walnut chest were hanging open. Clothes were strewn all around. Tad was busy packing his things in an old cloth satchel.

"Going away?" asked Mr. Lincoln as he opened the door and leaned casually against the door frame.

"Yes," said Tad.

"Is that so? Where are you headin' for first?"

"I'm not going far," said Tad.

"Farther than you can throw a bull by the tail?"

"I'm going over to live with Miss Sophia and the animals. Mamma won't let me do anything!"

"What will I do without you in Washington?"

Tad hesitated. "I don't want to go to Washington." He went on with his packing. He plunked a pair of heavy shoes on top of his best white shirt and closed the satchel.

"Say, by the way," said Mr. Lincoln, "you haven't had any supper, have you?"

"Nope," answered Tad.

"There's some cold roast duck in the cellar, and some mince tarts left from supper."

Tad stood holding the handle of the old satchel. He reflected on the charms of cold duck and mince tarts, as compared with the relative merits of moving in at once with an old goat.

"What do you say, Tadpole?"

"I guess I am kind of hungry," he said at last.

"I could eat something, myself," said Mr. Lincoln. The deep lines in his face relaxed, and his eyes twinkled. Men who had seen him pleading a case in a court of law had seen that same expression flit across his face when he knew he had scored a point with the jury.

The two of them tiptoed down to the kitchen and set a lamp on the drop-leaf table. They got a crock of milk from the cellar and the cold duck. The mince tarts were in the pantry, and Mr. Lincoln found a glass of black currant jelly to eat with the duck. Mr. Lincoln awkwardly sliced off great slabs from a round loaf of Mrs. Lincoln's homemade bread and spread them carefully with butter.

"Your mother is certainly a good cook," reflected Mr. Lincoln.

"Um-hum," said Tad around a mouthful of duck.

"It's our good luck, too, with the trouble she has keeping help these days. She must work every minute of the day to keep this household going by herself. I often wonder how she manages as well as she does. Likes things nice, too."

Tad said nothing. He opened his mouth as wide as he could to get it around the towering structure of a duck sandwich. The jelly squeezed out and stained his cheeks. The rich whole milk looked yellow in the hobnailed glass. Tad ran his fingers up and down the bumps on the outside of the glass.

Mr. Lincoln brought out some mince tarts from the pantry. The edges of folded pastry were crisp and brown. The fragrance of the spices within leaked out the little designs pricked into the top crust. Tad stretched his feet out before him, sighed deeply, and bit into his tart.

Mr. Lincoln also bit into a tart and closed his eyes. It was amazing how much better things tasted when they didn't come at the end of a big meal. He looked at Tad whose eyes were a little heavy. It was way past his bedtime.

"It says in the Bible," said Mr. Lincoln, "that a house divided against itself cannot stand."

"What do you mean, Papa?"

"Third chapter of Mark, I believe." Mr. Lincoln leaned back in his chair. He studied the ceiling with a long look. "Tad, that means that families have got to work together to be worth anything. That goes for nations, too. Can't everybody go off his own way. People have got to work together to accomplish anything worthwhile. I can't go to Washington and be a good President if you aren't working with me, and with Mamma and with Robert and Willie."

"You can't?"

"Mamma really has a tremendous job. She is going to need the help of all of us."

"I take out the garbage and beat the rugs."

"It's something deeper than that. You may be pretty young to understand. Your mother is a very fine woman, but she is keyed to a different pitch than we are. She grew up in a beautiful southern home. She always had things that were nice. Beautiful clothes, and people to wait on her. Living with us, especially with you and me, must be hard on her at times. You and I don't always remember how sensitive she is. I think she really suffers sometimes when we don't behave according to her standards."

"Papa, you never hurt anybody in your life!"

"Not deliberately, but I think I hurt your mother when I forget to wipe the mud off my boots, and leave my hat in a chair. You must remember that she is working much harder taking care of all of us than she ever worked in her life before. I think it is only fair that we try to help her all we can—in the little things, I mean. It's going to be very difficult for her to go to Washington and be a President's wife."

"I think she's going to like it."

"Perhaps. But you and I can do a lot to make it easier for her. We can try to protect her from the little things that upset her. You and I could shelter her a little—like—like the old green umbrella. She's going to need our help, Tad."

"Like the green umbrella?" Tad thought this over for a minute. Then he looked up and grinned. "I think I know what you mean. Can it be a secret between us?"

"Of course."

"I only wanted a goat, you know."

"You shall have one someday. Having one here isn't worth raising a storm. You see what I mean?"

"Mamma always hated storms, didn't she?" Tad picked up the last tart and ate it in two bites. "I'll be the best old umbrella you ever saw." He wiped the crumbs off his chin. "You mean no more fights with Caleb Norton?"

"I wouldn't encourage it."

"He's going to Washington, you know. His pa is going to work on a paper there."

"Um." Mr. Lincoln's face sobered. "I didn't know."

"I might have to punch him someday."

"Well, we'll handle that when the time comes. Now how about getting into bed, my little Green Umbrella?"

Tad went whistling up the stairs to unpack his flannel nightshirt from the old satchel. Then suddenly remembering the responsibilities of a good umbrella he stopped whistling and tiptoed. No use disturbing everybody in the place.

6 SLEEPER TRAIN

The snow squeaked beneath his heels as Tad walked along the cars toward the engine. His breath frosted the plaid muffler that shielded his face from the biting February wind. He passed the coal car and came alongside the engine.

He drew a deep breath. It was a big thing; no wonder they called it an "Iron Horse." The smokestack was almost the biggest part of all. It rose toward the sky like a huge inverted funnel. Smoke curled out of it now. The big black body of the engine was panting like a hunting dog on a leash, eager to be off.

There were two small wheels under the front end of the engine, and two big ones with countless spokes under the engineer's cab. A cowcatcher fanned out over the track ahead.

Suddenly the engineer released some steam, and Tad looked down to see the side of his pants were soaked by it. Almost at once it began to freeze on him. He could hardly bend his knee.

"Hey!" he shouted at the engineer. "Look what you've done!"

The engineer poked his head out of the window and laughed. "Better stand clear of this thing. Nasty disposition it's got. Good thing you have a lot of clothes on or you'd have been scalded." He disappeared again.

"Hey!" shouted Tad again. "Can I come up there by the fire and dry off? My mamma won't like it if my pants are froze."

The engineer appeared between the engine and the coal car.

"I guess you can," he said. "Come on up right here. I got a boy your size myself."

Tad climbed into the cab of the engine. It was a wonderland of levers and throttles. The fireman threw open the door to the firebox and began to shovel in coal. The fire became a roaring inferno. Black smoke belched from the funnel chimney. The heat was intense.

"You don't need to build it up for me," said Tad.

"For you? Say, I'm building up steam to take this train across the country. We're taking the President clear to Washington, you know." He threw in one more shovelful and slammed the iron door.

"Yes, I know," said Tad.

"Everybody, does, I suppose."

Tad's trousers began to steam dry in the intense heat of the engine cab.

"We're leaving in fifteen minutes," said the engineer, pulling out a big watch and studying it.

"Pressure is almost up," said the fireman. "Hey, young man, want to throw in a few shovelfuls of coal? Good practical way to get thawed out. I want to do some last minute greasing." He winked at the engineer and handed the big shovel to Tad.

"Sure, I'll shovel," said Tad, setting to work.

His face was soon covered with soot, and perspiration began to run down in streaks. He stopped to rest a minute and wiped his forehead on his sleeve.

"How do you make it start?" he asked the engineer.

"See this throttle here?"

"Yes."

"I give it a pull. It releases some of the steam into the cylinders above the front wheels. That steam forces the pistons back that are connected with the big driving wheels and around they go. Powerful thing, steam."

"Where do you get it?"

"We make it. There is water in that long cylindrical body of the engine. The water is heated by the fire and turned into steam. See this gauge?"

"Yes."

"Have to watch the gauge, or that steam in the boiler might build up enough pressure to blow us into the next county."

Tad resumed his work. "Kinda warm in here, isn't it?" He unwound his muffler and unbuttoned his coat.

"Yes, it is," said the engineer, "but that's not why we have to keep the windows open. We have to keep a lookout for signals along the way and for cows. They have absolutely no respect for the railroad's right-of-way. Why, one day when I was making the run from Springfield to Chicago, a cow got right in the middle of the track to chew her cud and ..."

"Hey, Tad! Tad Lincoln!" Caleb Norton's voice rose shrilly outside the engine.

"What do you want?" said Tad, poking his head out the window.

"So that's where you are. Your mother has been looking everywhere for you."

The engineer and the fireman looked at each other in amazement.

"You Tad Lincoln?" asked the fireman, hoping he had misunderstood. He took the shovel out of Tad's hands.

"Yes, sir," said Tad, buttoning up his coat.

The engineer was fumbling through his inner pockets for a clean handkerchief. Unearthing one, he began a major repair job on Tad's dirty face.

The fireman looked at his watch.

"Three minutes," he said.

"See this lever?" said the engineer to Tad.

"Yes."

"Give it a couple of quick pulls."

The shrill voice of a steam whistle cut the cold air. Tad jumped.

"Now if you give this rope a good hard pull, it'll start the bell ringing. Give people plenty of time to clear off the tracks. The whole town of Springfield must be down here just to see this train off."

The fireman shoveled in one more chunk of coal and slammed the iron door to the firebox. "To think I had the President's son shoveling coal for me!" He shook his head. "Just to think!"

"Didn't hurt me a bit," said Tad with a grin.

"Then we're friends?"

"Of course." Tad held out his hand, and the fireman took it in both of his.

"You want to come up here and see us again?" asked the engineer.

"I certainly do."

"We have a long stop in Indianapolis. Your father's going to make a speech. That will give us time to overhaul the engine. You come up here, and we'll treat you like a prince. We'll—we'll let you drive her across Indiana."

"I'll be here," said Tad, climbing down from the engine.

"Run like everything," said the engineer. "We don't want to leave you behind."

Tad's feet flew over the snow as he went back to the rear end of the train. He climbed aboard the last car and stood on the platform with his father. He looked out over a sea of sober faces. Some people were crying. That seemed strange. The distant clang of the engine bell made Tad's heart jump around in his stomach. In a minute the train would start. The steam would drive the pistons, and the big wheels on the engine would start to roll. Springfield would be left behind them.

Mr. Lincoln spoke to the people of Springfield in a sad, quiet voice:

"My friends, no one not in my situation can appreciate my feeling of sadness at this parting. To this place, and the kindness of you people, I owe everything. Here I have lived a quarter of a century, and have passed from a young to an old man. Here my children have been born, and one is buried. I now leave, not knowing when or whether ever I may return, with a task before me as great as that which rested upon Washington. Without the assistance of that Divine Being I cannot succeed. With that assistance I cannot fail. Trusting in Him who can go with me and remain with you, and be everywhere for good, let us confidently hope that all will yet be well. I bid you all an affectionate farewell."

In the silence that followed, the train lurched suddenly and began to move. Tad took hold of his father's hand. They stood together on the rear platform until the train reached the outskirts of the village. Tad caught a glimpse of Miss Sophia's little white house and the barn that was now the home of Blackie and the goat. A lump that he couldn't swallow rose in his throat.

Mr. Lincoln looked down at Tad. The sad lines of his face softened.

"Come with me," he said. "I have some surprising

things to show you. It's the most amazing thing you ever saw, this sleeper train."

"Is it more amazing than the steam engine?"

"Well, no, I guess not."

"I've been shoveling coal in the firebox." Tad looked up at his father and grinned, as they went into the parlor car on the rear end of the train.

"You have?"

"Yes, and I pulled the bell and blew the whistle. I made friends with the engineer and fireman. They're going to let me drive the train across Indiana."

"I begin to understand how you got that shadow along your chin."

Mr. Lincoln looked around the parlor car. Mrs. Lincoln and Willie had evidently gone on into the sleeper car ahead. Robert was busy writing a letter to the girl he left behind.

"You come with me," said Mr. Lincoln to Tad. "I'm going to wash your face and neck."

"On the train?"

"Of course. There's a little basin in the washroom at the end of the car, and water and towels and soap."

"There are?"

"Your mother is the only one of us who seems genuinely happy about leaving Springfield. We can't spoil her good time with a dirty neck, can we?"

Tad came out of the washroom with his face shining. He looked out across the rolling prairies of Illinois that were covered with snow. Springfield was gone. The engine with the big stack was roaring along toward the nation's capital. Chunks of soot brushed the window, little whispered messages from the men in the engine.

"Good thing they've got a strainer in that smokestack," thought Tad, "or whole big coals would come flying out and set somebody's barn on fire."

He sat down in one of the big chairs upholstered in flowered plush. He brushed his feet along the deep pile of the carpet. There had never been anything like this underfoot in his old house on Eighth Street. He studied the elaborate kerosene lamps that swung in brackets from the ceiling. Everything is so grand, he thought.

The train rocked quietly. The engineer blew the whistle. Two long blasts and two short ones.

Tad sank deeper into the chair and smiled to himself. It wasn't so bad to be leaving Springfield, not when the engineer and fireman were your good friends.

The porter came through announcing that supper was ready in the dining car. Tad and his father joined Mrs. Lincoln, Willie, and Robert in the Pullman car ahead.

"Where's the dining car?" asked Tad.

"Just ahead, I believe," said Mr. Lincoln.

"Well, if this is a sleeper train, where are the beds?"

"Right here. There are three or four dozen beds right here in this car." Mr. Lincoln waved his hand.

Tad looked up and down the plush covered seats. It looked to him as though everybody was going to have to sleep sitting up. That was all right with Tad. He knew he'd be too excited to sleep.

When it was time to go to bed, Tad kept an eye on the porter. He wanted to be sure and see where all the beds his father talked about came from.

Finally the porter came along to make up the berths. Tad watched every move. First he pulled the seats of the section together and pushed down the plush-covered backs to make a four-section mattress.

"Well," said Tad. "There is a place to lie down."

"Now you just wait a minute," said the porter. He took a big key from his pocket. He unlocked what looked to Tad like a curved bulge against the ceiling, and it dropped down to make an upper berth. Here in this upper berth were stored the pillows and blankets and clean sheets that the porter needed. With a few expert strokes he made up the two beds. Then he hung heavy green curtains from ceiling to floor. Now the beds were ready. He moved along the car making up all the berths. When he had finished, the aisle was just a canyon, green-walled with curtains.

7 DANGER AHEAD

Tad had been living on the train for four wonderful days. There was excitement around every curve. He had been busy, too. There was Jasper to look after in the baggage car, and he and Willie played a game of counting barns. Tad had driven the engine across Indiana, as the engineer had promised. And there was always the fun of going into the diner for meals.

Tad loved the look of the snowy white tablecloths, the sparkling glassware and silver, the squatty sugar bowl full of sugar, the milk slopping around in the glass as the train rocked. He loved the exciting feeling he got watching the country outside rush past the windows as fast as it could go.

Tad would never forget the first morning he went into the diner. He and Willie were up early, and the two of them went into the diner to see if there was any breakfast ready for them.

The jovial waiter in his white coat pulled Tad's chair out for him and shoved him against the table.

"What will you boys have for breakfast?" asked the waiter.

"Oatmeal?" said Willie.

"Oatmeal, yes, sir."

"I don't want oatmeal," said Tad.

"Well, what do you want the most of anything you could call to mind?"

"Pancakes! A big stack of pancakes with maple syrup and butter," said Tad. He didn't believe that there were pancakes in the little cubbyhole of a kitchen, but the waiter had asked him.

Tad had the surprise of his life when a few minutes later the waiter reappeared with a big stack of pancakes and syrup and butter. They were covered by a silver dome with a hole in the top of it out of which curled a thin tendril of fragrant steam. Tad put his finger over the hole and felt the moist warmth of the steam settle on it.

"Whatever are you doing?" asked Willie.

"Steam," said Tad with a sigh; "wonderful thing, steam."

"Well, eat your pancakes, for goodness sake!"

Tad took the lid off, and Willie continued to work on his big bowl of oatmeal without enthusiasm. With great care, Tad spread butter between each pancake in the stack. Then poured half a pitcher of maple syrup over the whole thing. Willie watched him closely. Finally he put down his spoon.

"Want a pancake?" asked Tad.

Willie set his oatmeal to one side and helped himself to a couple of the cakes. The waiter brought in a plate of little sausages. Then he brought hot muffins and milk.

"Nothing too good for the President's boys, that's what I think," said the waiter.

After breakfast Tad went to feed Jasper. Then he returned to Willie. Mrs. Lincoln was sick from the motion of the train, so Tad and Willie were left on their own. They had no trouble finding things to do in this small but exciting world on wheels that had become their home. And so, the day sped by.

Tad had been too busy to notice that he was seeing less and less of his father each day. Mr. Lincoln kept a little table set up in his section of the Pullman car and worked constantly. There were speeches to make at almost every stop. He had two bodyguards with him all the time, and there were countless people aboard the train. Like Mr. Lincoln, they worked long into the night.

When it began to get dark, the porter came into the President's car to light the kerosene lamps that swung from the ceiling. Tad and Willie were playing a game of chess.

"Where are we now?" asked Tad.

"Bless you. We are nowhere just now, sir. But we're coming into Philadelphia, the first thing you know."

67

"Is supper ready yet?" asked Tad.

"I believe it is," said the porter. Before the last word was out of his mouth, the chess game was upset and the boys were gone.

When they came back after supper, the berths were all made up, except the President's section across from Tad's and Willie's. He sat there working at his little table, a little island of light, surrounded by a sea of green curtains.

The boys did not disturb their father, but went right to bed. The porter held a little ladder for Tad to climb into the upper berth. Willie slept below.

It was hard to undress in the cramped quarters of an upper berth with the train rocking from side to side. Sometimes Tad didn't take off all his clothes. Shucks, he'd just have to put them all on again in the morning.

He lay listening to the noises of the train as it plowed along through the night. He could hear the engine above the rhythmic noise of the wheels on the steel rails. Tad felt a sense of snug security in that upper berth. He was shut off from all the rest of the world by those green curtains. He couldn't go to sleep. He turned from side to side. He was vaguely conscious of a rising crescendo of voices in his father's section across the aisle. They were disturbing him. Suddenly he sat up and listened.

"You have to listen to us, Mr. Lincoln." It was Colonel Ellsworth's voice. "It's a plot to kill you."

Tad peeked out between the curtains. His father did not seem disturbed. He continued to work on his speech for Philadelphia.

"He's the hardest man for a bodyguard to look after that I ever saw." One of the bodyguards spoke to another.

"That's because he is not afraid of anything," said Dr. Judd.

"How are we going to guard the life of a man who never has a thought for his own personal safety?" said the second bodyguard.

Lincoln continued to write.

"I've been in touch with detectives in New York,"

said John Hay. "They say the plan is to kill him in Baltimore—to stab him in the carriage as he rides from one station to the other."

"Rubbish," said Mr. Lincoln going on with his work.

"I have an old Scotch shawl and cap," said Dr. Judd. "I think he should wear them as a disguise. When we leave Philadelphia, the President in this disguise and I should go to Washington via a different route and fool them."

"That's it," shouted the bodyguard, "that's it! Leave us out of it altogether. It's our job to safeguard the President's life!"

"Gentlemen! Gentlemen!" said Mr. Lincoln, finally laying down his pen. "You all are making a confounded lot of noise for a man who is trying to write the most important speech of his career."

"There's a plot to kill you!"

"You fellows make me think of a farmer back in Indiana when I was a boy. He was riding his horse through a storm. It was a pitch-black night except when the lightning flashed. The thunder was terrific. It shook the earth. One sudden clap knocked him clean off his horse. He was scared to death. He knelt in the road and cried: 'Oh, Lord, let us have more light and less noise!' " Mr. Lincoln turned back to his work.

"He wants to know more about it, before he'll believe it," said Dr. Judd.

"What can we do with the man?" said the bodyguard.

Tad sat back in his berth, stunned. Somebody wanted to kill his father. It couldn't be. Not his father who had always been kind to everybody and everything, even turtles. Tad shivered slightly, and lay wide awake in the dim security of his upper berth.

A door slammed at the end of the car. Someone came running down the aisle. Tad peeked out of the curtains again. It was John Nicolay. "The whole ghastly plot is true!" he shouted. "I've just had a wire from Mr. Pinkerton in New York. It says the same thing. Baltimore. Stab in coach between stations."

"There's a little more light for you, Mr. President," said Dr. Judd.

"All right. All right. Get your shawl and bonnet."

"I still think we should go along, too," said the bodyguard.

Dr. Judd put his hand gently on Mr. Lincoln's shoulder. "Your life isn't really your own, now, you know. You belong to the people who believe in you and made you President. That's why we have to take care of you."

"A lot of ridiculous poppycock."

The men around Mr. Lincoln's small table left. The car quieted down and Lincoln continued to write his speech for Philadelphia. Tad lay back in his berth again. Finally he felt the train slowing down for Philadelphia. Mr. Lincoln stood up and gathered up his papers.

"Papa!" Tad whispered between the curtains.

"Why, son, are you awake?" Mr. Lincoln's kind eyes were on a level with Tad's as he stood in the aisle.

"Are you afraid, Papa?"

"No. I am not afraid of anything but God and the responsibility that war will put on my shoulders."

"Is God on our side, Papa?"

"God? I don't know that God ever has a hand in war, but I suppose he does. If so, it's pretty well up to us to see that we get on His side."

"You're not going on to Washington with us on this train, are you?"

"No, Tad."

"I want to go with you. I can take care of you."

Mr. Lincoln laughed his deep-throated laugh. Tad laughed, too. Nobody had anything to fear who could laugh like that.

"You can't go with me, son, but you can stay on here and be a great help to me."

"How?"

"By taking care of your mother. I am thinking she will need it more than I will." He kissed the face that was framed in the green curtains, and then tucked him in snugly. "I will see you at the White House." The curtains closed, and he was gone.

Before long, the train jolted to a stop, and Tad knew they were in Philadelphia. He knew his father was getting off the train. He resolved to be a help to his mother tomorrow. He would be her green umbrella.

The next day, the long train ride was almost over. Tad sat beside his mother as they drew into the out-skirts of the city of Washington. She sat erect in her fine new black coat and her new bonnet. Her shoulder twitched nervously.

"This is a fine way for the special presidential train to arrive," she said, "with no President."

"You wouldn't want him to take a chance of being stabbed in his carriage, would you?" asked Tad.

"Heavens, no! Not when I've got him this near to the White House."

The train was pulling into the station. "I wonder if there will be crowds to meet the train," said Mrs. Lincoln. Her shoulder twitched again.

"Oh, sure," said Tad. "Crowds and bands and people staring at us."

"Whatever will people think of me?" said Mrs. Lincoln. She straightened her bonnet, and braced herself for the ordeal of facing the Washington crowds for the first time.

Why, she's scared to death, thought Tad. He smiled up at his mother and slipped his hand into hers and held it tight.

8 DOUBLE TROUBLE

Tad and Willie sat on the top step of the great wide stairway of the White House. They said little, for an air of expectancy hung over them. Their father had told them to wait there for him.

"You two wait right there for me, so that I will know where you are," he had said. And he added, "I have a wonderful surprise for you," and disappeared into his study.

The country was at war. The boys had seen very little of their busy father in the last few months, and less of their mother. She was busy accumulating enough gowns to meet the social requirements of the wartime capital. Her maid, Lizzie Keckley, was an excellent seamstress, and Mrs. Lincoln kept her busy with satins and laces and hoops and fittings. The boys had made the most of their freedom. They had explored the White House from attic to cellar. They had played every game they could think of. Their own lives had not yet been touched by the war, although sometimes they could hear the guns booming across the river in Alexandria.

The boys sat patiently on the top step and watched the stream of people that poured in to see their father. There were politicians, men in uniform, women in tears. Mr. Lincoln saw everyone that could get past old Daniel at the door.

A lovely girl about sixteen came up the steps.

"Vinnie Ream!" cried the boys, jumping to their feet.

"Papa isn't going to pose for you now, is he?" asked Tad.

"I had hoped he would. I must finish that bust I am doing for the Capitol building."

"He's awfully busy," said Willie.

"Did you know that Robert is going away tomorrow to fight with General Grant?" said Tad as an idea struck him. He wasn't going to let a beautiful young sculptress keep his father from showing them the surprise.

"Robert? Going tomorrow?" Vinnie's face had a stricken look.

"That's right. No more Harvard for him," said Willie. "He got his uniform this morning."

"Yes," said Tad. "He's in the East Room now, strutting in front of a long mirror. He would like to tell you good-bye, I know." Tad looked as innocent as a cherub, as Vinnie picked up her hoopskirts in both hands and fled toward the East Room.

"Did Robert tell you he wanted to say good-bye to Vinnie?" asked Willie.

"Well," Tad hesitated. "No. He didn't tell me. But haven't you noticed the way Robert hangs around when Vinnie is working on that old head of Papa, and the way he looks! Mush! Anyway, every soldier wants to tell a beautiful girl good-bye. It makes them fight better."

"That's right."

"And who wants an old clay head of Papa, anyway?"

Just then Captain John Ericsson came through the door like a breath of fresh salt air. He was a frequent visitor at the White House.

"Well, well," he said in his booming voice. "What are you two fellows up to this morning?"

"We're just waiting for Papa," said Tad.

"He told us to wait right here for him," said Willie.

"Is that so?" said Captain Ericsson, sitting down on the steps with them. "Then I wait here, too." He had a delightful Swedish accent, and the boys loved to hear him talk. He was a man of about sixty. He was bald about halfway back on his head, but from there on, his heavy hair hung down over his collar. His chin was smooth shaven, but he made up for his lack of top hair by wearing shaggy sideburns that framed his jovial face like a fur parka.

"You aren't really going to build an iron ship, are you?" asked Tad.

"Indeed I am. The *Monitor* is going to be the first ironclad, steam-driven ship in the United States Navy, but I bet you it will not be the last."

"It'll sink if you build it of iron," said Willie.

"Don't tell me you think I am crazy, too. Everybody thinks so but your father. Thank heavens he had some experience with flatboats on the rivers of Illinois. He has often figured to a pound how much weight a flatboat could carry. He knows what I'm

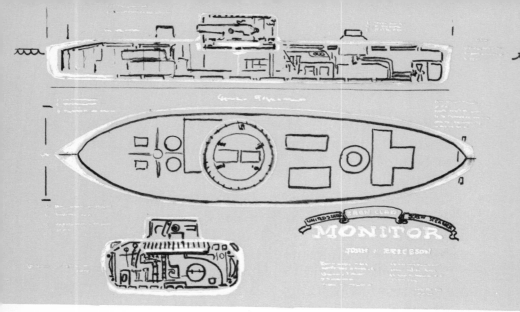

talking about. We can't let the *Merrimac* come out of Norfolk and sink any more of our frigates."

"Will the *Monitor* beat the *Merrimac?*" asked Tad.

"Yes, sir!" said Captain Ericsson. "Let me show you what a great battleship looks like." He pulled a roll of plans from his pocket and spread them out on the floor. The three of them knelt on the top step to study them.

"There," said Captain Ericsson, caressing the sheets. "A hundred and seventy-five feet from end to end— all armor-plated. It's built right flat on the water."

"Looks like an old flatiron without a handle," said Tad.

"What's that big round thing on the top?" asked Willie.

"That's the revolving gun turret. Two eleven-inch guns. We can run circles around the *Merrimac* and keep shooting all the time. We won't give her time to turn around and maneuver her guns into position."

"What makes it go? It looks funny without any sails."

"Steam."

"Same as a steam engine?" asked Tad. "I know about steam engines."

"Same thing," said Captain Ericsson. "And I have some wonderful new ideas about steam. I've been experimenting with it. As soon as the steam cools and condenses into water again, I send it back through the boiler again. It is already hot, so it doesn't have to be heated all over again. It's going to revolutionize steam engines, make them faster and more powerful."

The three figures on the top step were so intent on the plans of the *Monitor* that they did not see the tall figure that came along and stood looking over their shoulders at the drawings.

"I think if you turned it upside down and used that cheesebox for a keel, you might have something."

"Mr. President!" said Captain Ericsson.

"Papa!" cried Tad and Willie. "What is the surprise?"

"You all come with me, and you will see. Come along, John. There are some things about this *Monitor* I want to talk over with you."

The four of them went down the broad steps to the front door. Old Daniel swung it open for them. Mr. Lincoln stopped for a word with him, as he always did.

"How are you today, Daniel?"

"I am not good," sighed Daniel. "I got a misery in my back. I don't think I'm going to live much longer."

"Oh, come, come," said the President, slapping him affectionately on the shoulder. "You can't die, Daniel. Indeed you can't. That would leave me the homeliest man in Washington."

"That's right, sir," said Daniel chuckling.

The four of them walked around the driveway toward the stables. The new gardener was working on the rose beds. He didn't look up as they passed, but continued working steadily with his hoe. He was the only person on the White House property that the boys had not made their friend.

Suddenly Tad and Willie broke into a run. They had caught sight of something in the stable yard; a

pair of goats hitched to a little red wagon, and a pony all saddled and ready for a rider.

Tad stood looking at the goats. He couldn't say a word. He looked up at his father, his eyes swimming with tears of joy.

"That's right," said Mr. Lincoln. "The goats are for you, and the pony is for Willie. May you have many hours of fun."

Willie climbed into the saddle and walked the pony around the yard. Tad sank on his knees and tried to gather both goats into his arms at once. Jasper sat on the fence and made his own crow comments about the whole affair.

Mr. Lincoln turned to Captain Ericsson. "Never knew a boy to want anything like Tad has wanted a goat. I wanted to see his face when he got out here, that's why I made them wait half the morning for me."

Mr. Lincoln put the plans of the *Monitor* in his pocket and watched Tad climb into the little cart and pick up the reins. Tad rode around the stable yard a couple of times to make sure the goats would respond to the reins like a pair of horses. He pulled up before his father.

"Mamma won't care if I have these goats?"

"I am sure she won't, now that you have a stable to keep them in and a groom to keep them clean."

"I don't need a groom. I'm going to take every bit of care of them myself, and they won't smell a bit. Can I give you a ride?" There was such appeal in the question that Mr. Lincoln could not resist.

"Well, just around to the door. I have to get back to my work." He sat down in the small cart. By pulling his knees up against his ears, he managed to get his feet in, too. Captain Ericsson laughed his booming laugh and waved to them as they started with such a jerk that the President's head snapped back on his neck.

The goats pranced along toward the front door of the White House. They picked their feet up with pride as though they were aware of the importance of their load.

Suddenly one of the windows on the second floor of the White House flew open and Mrs. Lincoln cried out, "Mr. Lincoln! What are you doing out there in that ridiculous cart? Get out of there at once before somebody sees you."

Tad stopped the cart, and Mr. Lincoln got out and stretched his legs. He patted Tad affectionately on the head. " 'There must be an hour somewhere where a man could be happy all his life,' " he quoted, " 'if he could only find it . . .' There, run along, Tad, and love your goats to death."

With this means of transportation, Washington was a new and bigger world for Tad. He became a familiar figure on the city streets in his little red cart. Every day he went to see his friend, the organ grinder, who had a most intelligent monkey. Often he went to the fish wharf which always fascinated him.

One day as he was riding along Pennsylvania Avenue, a familiar voice hailed him. He stopped and looked around. It was Caleb Norton.

"Come on, get in, I'll give you a ride," said Tad generously. It was the first time Tad had seen Caleb in Washington, although he knew Mr. Norton was in town stirring up trouble with his newspaper.

"So you don't think you're too smart to ride with just plain folks, like me?" said Caleb.

"Why, no," said Tad. "I'm just plain folks, too."

They rode on in silence.

"Well, said Caleb, "I know I wouldn't want to live in the old White House if I had to live with a spy."

"What do you mean?"

"Don't you know that important papers have been disappearing from the White House?"

"No."

"The South is getting valuable information."

"They are not."

"They are, too."

"Who would send secret information from the White House?" said Tad, sticking out his jaw.

"Your mother. That's who."

Tad stopped the goats and looked at Caleb. "What are you talking about? You can't prove what you say is true."

"You can't prove it isn't. She's got a brother in the Confederate Army, hasn't she?"

"Why, yes."

"Well—and now a set of plans of the *Monitor* has disappeared from your father's pocket."

Tad looked at Caleb, stunned.

"Who'd go through your father's pockets but your mother?"

"She's in New York buying clothes."

"Maybe that's what she said. I bet she took those plans of the *Monitor* with her. My pa thinks so. He's going to print a story about her in his paper tomorrow."

"Get out!" screamed Tad.

Caleb scrambled out, and Tad was right after him. He was mad enough to put power into the right jab to the chin that sent Caleb sprawling.

"Sometimes a fellow has to fight," said Tad between his teeth. "Get up!"

Caleb got up and ran. "You just read the papers, that's all," he called back over his shoulder.

Tad wiped the perspiration off his forehead on his sleeve. He turned around to get into his little red cart, but the goats had run away and taken the cart with them.

9 THE GREEN UMBRELLA

Tad couldn't see the goats anywhere. He ran back home as fast as he could go.

When he got there, it looked as though the war had broken out on the south lawn. The goats had cut loose from the cart and were running wild through the rose garden and the pansy beds. The gardener was chasing them with his hoe, and there was murder in his eye.

Tad finally managed to catch the goats and hang onto them by their collars. They stood as quiet as lambs with their master.

The gardener came up to Tad. There was a wild look in his eyes. "Maybe he's crazy," thought Tad.

"You scared them," said Tad defiantly. "You can't ever catch an animal when you're chasing it with a hoe."

"I'm going to kill those goats." It was a hoarse whisper, full of threat. "First chance I get, I'm going to shoot them!"

"No," cried Tad, his eyes wide. This was the first time he had ever heard the gardener say more than three words.

"Look at my rose garden. Those goats ruined my rose bed."

"Shucks," said Tad, "just a few old roses. You got lots of better flowers around here."

"Nobody touches that rose bed!" The gardener's eyes narrowed to slits, and Tad backed up a step or two. "Nobody touches that rose bed, see?" He pointed to a small spot under the trellis where the goats had plowed the earth up rather thoroughly. "I'm going to court-martial those goats and shoot them myself."

Tad turned and fled. He hung on to the goats' collars and led them toward the house, leaving the cart where it was. Through the White House door he went with the goats and up to the safety of his own room. When he saw the animals settle down comfortably in the middle of his bed, he remembered with infinite relief that his mother was in New York.

His mother! She needed some protection now if she ever did. He was her green umbrella, so it was up to him. He had to think of something fast. Tomorrow would be too late. If that story were printed in Mr. Norton's paper, whether it was true or not, she would be an outcast in the Washington society that was so important to her. Tad admitted to himself that his mother had some queer traits, but treachery was not one of them. She was loyal to Mr. Lincoln, that he knew, but how to prove it was what worried him.

Tad and Willie ate their supper in Willie's room and talked over the situation. They worked out a plan, deciding not to involve their father in it, because he had almost more troubles already than one man could shoulder.

"Funny, isn't it," said Willie with his mouth full

of chicken pie, "how when there's a war, everybody gets in it. Everybody has to help in some way."

"That's right."

"Papa's in it. Robert's gone to fight, and now we're in it, too."

"And we've got to do our part," said Tad. "We've got to."

The boys went to bed as usual, so as not to excite any curiosity. Tad had a little trouble getting his goats to settle down under the bed. He would get one tucked away and the other would be back up on the soft mattress.

Finally Tad gave up. He let both goats have the bed, and he curled up on the little horsehair sofa. He didn't sleep. He was waiting until it was completely dark outside.

The last of the lingering summer twilight faded from the sky. The stars appeared. Tad counted them. "When I can see ten," he thought, "then it will be time to go."

The door of his room opened slowly. The tall, gaunt figure of his father was silhouetted in the doorway against the candlelight in the hall. He came into the room quietly closing the door behind him, and sat down on the edge of the bed. He sighed wearily.

"Are you asleep, my little Tadpole?"

There was no answer from the bed.

"Well, again I am too late to hear your prayers, but at least," he bent his head down tenderly, "I can kiss you good-night." Contact with the furry bristles of a goat's face brought him to his feet in the middle of the room.

"Great Snakes!" he shouted. "What have you got in bed with you?"

Tad howled with laughter and rolled off the sofa. His father lit a candle and surveyed the room. Then his own hearty laughter overflowed and bounced around against the walls. All the pent-up worry that had bowed him down for weeks was lifted for a minute. He could always laugh best when the joke was on himself. With tears of laughter trickling down the deep lines of his face, he sat down on the sofa and pulled Tad onto his lap.

"I know this is a nice big house," he said, "and

Washington is crowded. But if you want to take in roomers, you should get references. I think these fellows are scoundrels."

"They aren't scoundrels," said Tad.

"What are they?"

"They're fugitives."

"From what?" asked the President.

"From a court-martial. The gardener is going to shoot them for digging up his garden."

"Nonsense."

"Honest."

"Well," said Mr. Lincoln, "that's pretty serious. Come to my office in the morning, and I will write them a pardon."

"Papa," said Tad, "is it true that the plans for the *Monitor* were stolen?"

"Several important papers have disappeared. The secret service is working on it. Don't bother your little head about that."

Tad was silent. Then there was somebody taking things.

"What makes you ask a question like that?" said Mr. Lincoln.

The door to Tad's room opened a crack. Willie's hushed voice said, "It's all dark, Tad, are you ready to go?"

"What's going on here?" asked Mr. Lincoln.

Willie came into the room.

"Oh," he said, "I didn't know . . ."

"Papa," said Tad, "we think we know where those stolen papers might be."

"What!" Mr. Lincoln jumped into the middle of

the room. "You children can't know anything about that. You'd better get into bed where you belong."

Tad took hold of his father's hand and looked up into his face.

"This is awful important," he said. "Would you just stay here and mind the goats for a few minutes for us? Willie and I have work to do."

"You might get hurt. People who steal papers are pretty desperate characters."

Tad and Willie were edging toward the door. "We'll be right back," said Tad, and they were gone. Barefooted and in their little white nightshirts, they flew down the hall and disappeared.

Mr. Lincoln paced the floor and eyed the goats, laughing to himself from time to time.

Time went slowly. Mr. Lincoln found the quiet companionship of a pair of goats rather restful. They had no demands to make of him. They wanted no favors. They didn't even have any ideas to submit on how they thought the war should be run. He paced the floor and thought out a lot of his problems. As time passed he began to be alarmed about the boys. He opened the door and looked out into the hall. There was no sign of them. He tried looking out of the window, but the night was black and the shadow of the house hid everything below. Why had he let them go? Those boys! They had been busy about some monkey business or other ever since they arrived in Washington. Mr. Lincoln tried to curl up on the black sofa to get a little rest.

Soon he heard the boys coming. They burst into the room, triumphant. They had mud on their feet, mud up to their elbows, mud on their nightshirts.

"We got it!" They were carrying a black tin box.

"I never liked that man, even before the goats came," said Tad.

"What man?" asked Mr. Lincoln.

"That new gardener."

"What are you talking about? And look at you! Mud!"

"We got the stolen papers."

"Get in there and wash—you what?" Mr. Lincoln couldn't believe his ears.

"Got the stolen papers," said Tad simply.

"Let me see that box." Mr. Lincoln brushed the mud off it and opened it. "As I live," he said, "so you did."

Mr. Lincoln sat down and faced his sons. "All right," he said, "now start from the beginning."

The boys looked at each other. There was silent agreement between them not to mention their mother.

"Well," said Tad, taking a deep breath, "I was thinking about how somebody must be taking things and sending information to the enemy. When that gardener came after me with the hoe, and made such a fuss about his old rose garden, 'specially right under the trellis, I decided he was the one who had been taking things, and that was where they were hidden. Nobody would get so mad at goats just for digging."

"Go on."

"And anyway, people that raise flowers are kind and gentle. He was wrong all around. That's all there is to it. We went out and dug around ourselves, and look what we found! It's his all right."

Mr. Lincoln went to the door and spoke to one of his secret service men.

"Will they arrest him?" asked Willie.

"Yes, at once."

"And can the goats go back in the barn tomorrow, and will all this be in the papers?" said Tad.

"I'm sure of it."

"In Mr. Norton's paper, too?"

"Of course, why?"

"Pretty important, that's all."

"Now you boys get cleaned up. Then both of you better sleep in Willie's room for the night. And get those goats out of here, first thing in the morning. Goats don't belong in the house, and furthermore, your mother is coming home tomorrow."

"Green umbrella," said Tad grinning at his father. "I'll have the goats out early."

"By the way," said Mr. Lincoln, pausing at the door, "I think you two heroes should be rewarded for your good work. I appoint you both honorary lieutenants in the Union Army."

"With uniforms?" said Tad.

"Certainly."

"Hurrah!" shouted the boys.

"Report to me in the morning," said Mr. Lincoln.

"Yes, sir!" The boys clapped their muddy heels together and saluted their commander-in-chief.